THE
METER MAN

STEVEN E. WINTERS

authorHOUSE®

AuthorHouse™ LLC
1663 Liberty Drive
Bloomington, IN 47403
www.authorhouse.com
Phone: 1-800-839-8640

Published by AuthorHouse   08/15/2014

ISBN: 978-1-4969-3369-0 (sc)
ISBN: 978-1-4969-3368-3 (e)

Library of Congress Control Number: 2014914754

"...true evil needs no reason to exist, it simply is, and feeds upon itself."

E.A. Bucchianeri

Author Notes

I decided to briefly step away from my 'A Knight in the Ville' series. It is easy to write about Sistersville, WV, because I grew up there. But I needed a challenge. So I created a fictional story in a state I have never visited…Kentucky.

The entire writing process is a blast. The fun comes from creating the characters. The excitement comes from watching them become 'real'. As the story takes shape, I find my imagination churning out numerous plot twists and turns. I never plan an ending to a story, so even I am surprised when I reach it.

As with my 'A Knight in the Ville' stories, I like to end each chapter with a tease. I truly enjoy books that make you want to keep reading. I hope that is the case here. While this story is longer than my first three books, it is still relatively short. That is my style. For better or worse, I'm okay with that. I maintain that a good read shouldn't take a week to finish. Of course, determining whether this work qualifies as a good read is up to you, isn't it?

Writing brings a calmness and joy that is difficult to describe. The calmness comes during the writing phase itself, and the joy comes when a person like yourself reads my book and enjoys it. Of course, between the calmness and the joy, there is the grueling job of editing!

My editor is tough and never holds back on his criticism of my manuscripts. I happen to prefer that, because it makes me a better writer. Besides, if you can't take criticism, you will not last long as a writer. When he returned this manuscript to me after the first draft, he said, "I could tell early on that this story was disturbing, and at some point was going to make me feel uncomfortable. It did!"

You have been warned……

Other Books by Steven E. Winters

A Knight in the Ville – Why the Babies Cry
A Knight in the Ville – The December Dark
A Knight in the Ville – Beneath the Bricks

Coming in November 2014

A Knight in the Ville – Grave Concerns

*Available in paperback and ebook

PROLOGUE

Please forgive me if my handwriting is a little shaky. My fingers are wracked with pain, and the pen tends to skid away at times. I can control my shaking wrist for a while, but my grip is not too good. Like the rest of me, my hand is feeble and breaking down with old age.

Old age…now that makes me laugh! But it's a laugh that hurts my throat as it rises to my lips, gritty with the sands of irony and reality. You see, I am not old. You would call me a liar if you could see my face---take me as some crazed, old codger gone left of his right mind. I am quite sane, my friend.

My name is Ned Waters. I am writing this journal as a last will and testament. I don't have anything to leave behind, except this story. But a man should leave something behind, just to show he was here.

It's dreadfully hot in this little cabin tonight. I could turn on the box fan, but it requires electricity, and I'll be damned if I give him the satisfaction of using any more of his devil juice! I'm writing by candlelight, and I won't use any more electricity until I finish what I have to say.

See, up here in Devil Hollow, you pay for the power you use. You can use all you like, or very little, but in the end, you will pay. I'm praying that my body will hold out until I finish this.

Hopefully, the Meter Man will stay away and not come around looking for a payment anytime soon. I have so little left to give...and he always takes too much. This is my story....

CHAPTER ONE

"Ned! Get your ass in here!"

Ned Waters rose from his desk and strode quickly toward the office of his boss, Mike Evans. Mike sounded excited, and it was rare to hear that particular emotion in the offices of the Kentucky Bureau of Statistics.

"What is it, Mike?"

"These numbers!" Mike said as he held up a sheet of paper. "Have you seen these numbers?"

Ned took the printout from Mike and studied it for a few seconds. "Wow, are these correct, Mike?"

"That's what we need to find out. Get with Sara and have her cross- reference these numbers with the Field Research Department. I want to know if they are real, or if someone goofed!"

Ned nodded and slowly walked back to his desk. In his twenty years with the bureau, he had seen a few odd things, but this seemed to top them all. He picked up his phone and buzzed Sara Eckels on the intercom. She picked up right away, which didn't surprise Ned. There wasn't always a lot to do at the bureau.

"What's up, stud?" Sara asked.

"Why do you always flirt with me when you know I don't date Rednecks?" Ned replied.

"Very funny! What do you want?"

"Come to my desk, my dear Watson. We have a mystery to solve!"

Ned hung up the phone and studied the sheet again. He began to suspect that one of the census workers had failed to do their job. According to the data sheet, there were one hundred and fifty people living in Devil Hollow, Kentucky, and not one of them was over the age of fifty-five. That was impossible. You could walk down any random street in the United States and find at least one person over the age of fifty-five. Ned shook his head and reached for his coffee mug.

Sara Eckels arrived a few minutes later and lowered herself into the chair in front of Ned's desk. She was a recent graduate of the University of Louisville, and was a very attractive girl. She had piercing blue eyes and long, blonde hair that sat on top of a slender, athletic body. Ned found it difficult to sway his eyes from her long legs as she crossed them and smoothed down her pleated skirt.

"My eyes are up here, Ned!" Sara said as she pointed toward her face.

Ned blushed, picked up the data sheet, and handed it to Sara. "Here's the mystery. Do you notice the maximum age of all these people?"

Sara glanced at the sheet, and handed it back to Ned. "So, it looks like whoever we hired to do the census in Devil Hollow didn't actually go there." Sara said.

"Correct," Ned replied. "This is common, since we hire part-time help to deliver the census sheets. Sometimes they simply pocket the money and turn in false documentation."

"They were kinda lazy in this case," Sara said with a laugh.

"Yes, I agree. At least they could have varied the ages a little."

"So, what do you want me to do, Ned?"

"Call down to Field Research and see if you can find out who was paid to distribute the census sheets in Devil Hollow, then see if we can contact that person."

"Will do, Sherlock!" Sara stood and walked away, and Ned caught himself following her with his eyes.

Gotta stop that old man. She's half your age, Ned told himself. He loosened his tie, laced his fingers behind his head, and closed his eyes as he leaned back in his chair. He thought back to when he'd been closer to Sara's age. He had been a star running back for the Kentucky Wildcats in college, but a knee injury had derailed his career at the end of his junior year. So he'd focused on his studies and had begun to plan for a career that would never include playing football on Sundays. He'd never envisioned that 'career' would have been spent behind a desk.

This job was about as far away from the excitement of playing football as you could get. Ned spent day after day and week after week crunching numbers and responding to data requests from various Kentucky businesses and agencies. Advertisers were their biggest customers; they were looking for which areas had the highest target age groups for the products they were promoting. Still, it was a good job with state benefits, which would allow Ned to retire at an earlier age than most people.

Once in a while an interesting case would pop up, and Ned would be sent out into the field to investigate. He hoped this would be one of those cases, because other than occasionally seeing Sara, being inside every day was a tedious existence.

CHAPTER TWO

S ara Eckels was smiling when she
returned to her office after meeting with
Ned Waters. Since she'd begun working at the
bureau one year ago, she had been dropping
subtle hints to Ned that she was interested in
him, but today was the first indication he had
given that he'd found her attractive. She had felt
a warm flush in her face when she had caught
him peeking at her legs. She almost felt sorry
now that she had chastised him. Maybe a longer
look would have made him more interested.

Since she'd been a young schoolgirl in
Owensboro, Kentucky, Sara had been aware of
Ned's football exploits. He had played football
at the same high school she'd attended, and
his pictures and trophies were still displayed
in the main hallway. Even though it had been
over twenty years since Ned had graduated, his
legendary status was still evident on campus.

When she'd graduated from college, she had
hoped to land a job with the Bureau of Statistics

just to be close to her hero. Although Ned had obviously aged from the photos she had walked by every day in high school, he was still a very handsome man. Standing six feet tall with large shoulders and Brad Pitt-type facial features, he still drew looks from young women. Sara had heard the office whispers among the women at the bureau about Ned's exploits, but they had not fazed her. Instead, they had given her hope that she might have a chance to date him.

Sara tried to set aside her personal feelings and concentrate on the task she had been assigned. If she did a good job, maybe Ned would notice her more. She called down to the Field Research Department and spoke with the supervisor. Within fifteen minutes, she received an e-mail with the name and address of the census worker who had been assigned to Devil Hollow. *Hmm… no phone number? Guess I'll have to pay him a visit.*

Sara pulled a company credit card from her desk drawer and called for a taxi. She thought about calling Ned to see if he wanted to go with her to check on the worker, but she decided against it. She didn't want him thinking that she couldn't handle a simple investigation.

The taxi arrived in front of the building ten minutes later. Sara opened the door and settled into the back seat. It was a short drive to the address she had been given. She paid the driver with her company credit card and added a five-dollar tip from her purse. After exiting the taxi, she immediately regretted not bringing Ned along. She was on a street with a row of old, rundown townhouses, half of which appeared deserted. There were broken window panes in one of them, and some yellow "DO NOT ENTER" tape was draped across the entrance to another.

Sara leaned into the open passenger window of the taxi and told the driver to wait for her. She walked over to the townhouse that matched the address she had and walked up the four steps to the front door. *At least this one looks clean,* she thought. She rang the bell, and a few seconds later, a pudgy, middle-aged man opened it. He squinted into the sunlight and raised his hand to shield his eyes.

"Can I help you?"

"Yes, sir. I'm Sara Eckels from the Kentucky Bureau of Statistics. Are you the Mr. Jim Johnson we hired to do the census in Devil Hollow two years ago?"

The man nodded. "I reckon I am. Why?"

"Well, sir, we were checking the data from the forms you turned in, and we found an irregularity."

"Oh? What would that be?"

Sara began to feel a little uncomfortable but continued, "Well sir, according to those forms, no one in Devil Hollow is over the age of fifty-five. We found that to be…well…odd."

Johnson rubbed his chin thoughtfully. "I suppose that is a mite odd."

"Sir, did you deliver those census forms to Devil Hollow? I hate to ask you, but, with this information, it seems that you may not have."

Johnson looked at her for a moment before speaking. "Young lady, there ain't no one who can get into Devil Hollow. The old bridge was torn down years ago."

"Then how did you deliver the census forms, Mr. Johnson?"

"I took them to the old river bridge road, right where it forks with old Route 22. A man comes down there from the mountain every two weeks to pick up and drop off mail for the folks who live in Devil Hollow. The mailman told me that's the only way to get stuff in there."

"So you did not personally deliver the forms?"

"No, Ma'am. But I did go back to the fork and pick them up two weeks later. The same fella that took 'em brought 'em back."

"I see. Did you check the forms to make sure they were correctly filled out?"

"Yep," Johnson answered, nodding. "I did, and all of 'em were completed."

"So you didn't notice the fact that no one in Devil Hollow was over the age of fifty-five?"

"Wasn't my job! All they told us in the training was to make sure each of the categories had a mark in the column of circles under it. All of 'em did."

"Thank you, Mr. Johnson. I appreciate your cooperation."

As she turned to leave, he said "You wouldn't have a few spare dollars on you for an old man, would ya?"

"I suppose you'll be using it for food?" she replied as she noted his stained flannel shirt.

"Well, I could use a cold drink, if ya know what I mean."

She pulled out a ten-dollar bill, handed it him, and then went down the steps and opened the taxi door.

"Oh, lady! There's just one more thing!" Johnson yelled to her from his doorway.

"Yes, Mr. Johnson?"

"You say none of them folks in Devil Hollow is over fifty-five?"

"That's correct, Mr. Johnson."

"Well, that's odd, 'cause the fella that met me had to be in his seventies!"

CHAPTER THREE

S ara returned to her office and typed up the information she had received from Mr. Johnson. Technically, he had carried out his duties as a census taker, so there was not going to be a simple solution to this mystery. She figured that it had to have been a joke. She knew that the Kentucky mountain people didn't care much for the government. The most likely scenario was that, when they had received the forms, they had decided to play a little trick on the state by falsifying their ages. Mountain life might be hard, but it couldn't possibly be so hard that no one lived past the age of fifty-five!

The phone on her desk rang, startling her. "Hello?"

"Hey there, Redneck! Did you solve the case yet?"

"You're just a bundle of laughs, Ned Waters! You should take your act to Comedy Central."

"I might do that! So, what have you found out?"

She told Ned the details of her visit with Mr. Johnson. "I'm sending you the report via e-mail attachment right now."

"Great. I'll be sure to read it first thing in the morning. It's five o'clock Watson, time to go home."

She looked at the clock on her desk; she hadn't noticed the time. "Oh, okay. Well, see you in the morning Holmes!"

"Oh, and Sara…good job! Have a nice night."

She smiled and hung up the phone. It wasn't often that she heard words of praise. She quickly gathered her things and rushed out to the parking lot, hoping to run into Ned as he left for the day. She was disappointed to see that his red BMW was already gone. *Bum knee my ass,* she thought. No one could ever accuse a Kentucky state employee of being slow when the clock struck 5:00 p.m.

The drive home was uneventful. The traffic was bad, but that was to be expected when you send everyone home at the same time every day. Sara laughed at the road-ragers who changed lanes every few seconds in the hope that someway, somehow, it would deliver them home to their cold beer faster. She had learned to use the time as a way to unwind. Placing the latest Green Day CD into her car stereo, she happily sang along with the lyrics as she slowly made her way home.

Sara opened her apartment door and was pleased that the vanilla air freshener she had purchased at the grocery store over the weekend was working well. She inhaled the aroma, kicked off her shoes, and headed to the fridge. The wine she had also selected at the store should have been properly chilled by now. She removed the bottle from the fridge, popped the cork, poured half a glass, and then shrugged her shoulders and continued pouring until the goblet was full. She carried the glass into the bathroom and began running a hot bath.

Sara stepped out of her skirt and panties and then removed her blouse and bra. She tested the bath water with her toes before sliding into the tub with a sigh of contentment. There was just something about a hot bath that relaxed her more than anything else. Maybe it was the warmth of the water, or maybe it was the glass of wine that always accompanied her. Either way, it was an experience that she began looking forward to every work day as quitting time neared.

As she sipped her wine, Sara began to let her mind drift back to Ned Waters. Even though it probably meant nothing to him, the words 'good job' meant the world to her. Sara had been born in the tiny town of Sistersville, WV. Her biological father had died when she'd been two years old. Although he had never married her mom, they had lived together until his death. When Sara had been eight years old, her mom had married. Her stepfather had been a boozer and an abuser. He'd resented Sara from the start, even telling her (when her mom hadn't been around) that she'd been a bastard child. When Sara had begun to bloom into a young woman, the verbal abuse had stopped…and the physical abuse had begun.

Sara could still smell the stench of alcohol on her stepfather's breath as he would paw at her young body. She'd always pretended to be asleep when he would sneak into her room in the middle of the night. The memory of his hands groping her tiny body still haunted her. It was only after he'd begun abusing her mother that those late-night visits had stopped for good. A young Sistersville police officer named Curtis Knight had arrested her stepfather for beating her mother, and after several court hearings and interviews with social services, Sara and her mom had moved to Owensboro to start over. Sara had heard somewhere that her stepfather had been killed while in prison. Deep down, she was glad.

As the memories flooded back, Sara reached down and pulled the drain plug. *Enough of that!* She stood up, toweled off, and then slipped on the soft white cotton robe that hung by the tub. She walked to the kitchen and refilled her glass. A simple compliment from a man whom she idolized had opened up the floodgates of pain; such was the depth of old wounds.

Sara walked into the living room and switched on the TV. There was a special report about the University of Kentucky extending the contract of their basketball coach. *Oh please!* Sara laughed. As a graduate of the University of Louisville, she had a keen dislike for the Wildcats, in spite of the fact that Ned Waters had played football there. She stretched out on the sofa and, using the remote, flipped through several channels until she found an episode of Appalachian Pickers. The bad memories, the interview with Mr. Johnson, and even Ned Waters faded from her mind as she watched her favorite pickers buying antique treasures. By 9:00 p.m. she was fast asleep.

CHAPTER FOUR

Ned stopped off at the China Wok restaurant on the way home and ordered their General Tso chicken. As he sat at the drive-through window, waiting on his order, he opened the glove box in his BMW and pulled out a bottle of antacid. When he was in college, he could eat a large pizza with all the toppings right before bedtime and never miss a second of sleep. Now, anything with a little spice in it required him to coat his stomach with medicine before eating it. Such was the bitter reality of growing older.

After receiving his dinner from the drive-through, Ned steered his car back onto the interstate and let the events of the day run through his mind. The statistical data he had received from his boss had made no sense. When Sara had told him the results of her interview with the former census worker, things had been no clearer than before. All she'd really seemed sure of was that the man had carried out his job duties, and hadn't been trying to hide anything about the forms he had distributed to Devil Hollow. Ned shifted into a lower gear and pulled his BMW into the local ABC liquor store.

"How's it going, Ned?" the cashier said with a big smile as Ned entered the store.

"Just another day in paradise, Joe. Bag me up a Johnny Walker Red?"

"Sure thing!"

Ned pulled out his wallet and paid the cashier. "See you in two days, Joe."

Ned returned to his car and placed the whiskey in the backseat. He hesitated for a moment before pulling out the bottle of antacids again. *Better make sure.* He knew that the spicy chicken and alcohol would not mix well; he needed to protect his stomach.

The food was still piping hot in the foil takeout tray when Ned opened it at his kitchen table fifteen minutes later. He picked the broccoli spears out, tossed them aside, and then dove into the tasty meal. He was starving. He had skipped lunch, preferring to use the one-hour break to catch a nap in his car. Mondays were always difficult for him. No matter how many years he had been working this Monday-through-Friday dayshift job, he still found it difficult to go to bed at a decent hour. After sleeping in all weekend, he seldom slept more than four or five hours on Sunday nights.

He ate quickly and without any attempt at table manners. As he scooped the last bite of rice into his mouth, he felt the sweat beading on his forehead. *Whew! Now that was a spicy dish!* He grabbed one of the paper napkins from the plastic takeout bag and wiped his forehead, mouth, and chin. *Now for a little desert!* He grabbed the whiskey bottle, walked over to the fridge, plopped some ice cubes into a glass, and poured himself a heaping portion of the liquor. Taking the bottle with him, he headed into the living room.

As with every room in his spacious condo, Ned's living room was decorated with memories of his stellar football career. Of particular pride was the large gold trophy sitting on the mantel above the fireplace. It proclaimed him as the Southeastern Conference Offensive Player of the Year. He had been second in the country in rushing yards that year. It was also a bittersweet reminder because it was the last trophy or award he had won before his debilitating injury.

He slowly walked over to his desk and turned on his computer. As it flickered to life, he took a sip of his drink and then typed in the password to his e-mail account. There were a few requests for him to speak at luncheons, and several more asking him to sign autographs at some car dealerships. Even after twenty years, such requests were still frequent. Ned made a good living from these engagements, some of which paid up to $5,000. They helped to keep him living in the lap of luxury, which he certainly could not do on his state salary.

He signed off without responding to any of the e-mails. He would forward them to his agent later. As he took another sip of his drink, he walked over to the telephone and checked his messages. Six telemarketers had called. *So much for having an unlisted number,* he thought with a smirk. He stood by the window for a moment, staring into the darkness, before retiring to his recliner. As he sat there, the stark reality of being single began to creep into his mind. After all those years of being a star, he was now very much alone. Gone were the accolades and cheers. Gone were the magazine covers and constant requests for interviews. Now, it was just the occasional autograph signing or speaking engagement.

Ned took a long drink and closed his eyes. The alcohol helped him remember the good times, but it also accentuated the bad. Even if he had been a bust in the pros, being a first-round draft pick would have made him rich for life. Nowadays, most of the first round picks were signing deals for ten million dollars or more. Ned allowed his fingers to run down to his left knee. He rubbed it gently, feeling the scar tissue from the operation. He took another long pull on his drink and stood up. *Woulda, coulda, shoulda! It doesn't matter now.* Taking the bottle with him, he shuffled off to the bathroom to take a long hot shower.

CHAPTER FIVE

Sara arose early the next morning with a stiff neck. She had slept for several hours on the sofa before waking up and shuffling off to bed. Her head must have been at an odd angle on the armrest of the sofa when she'd drifted off the night before. After brushing her teeth, she grabbed a few aspirin from the medicine cabinet and washed them down with a cup of water. After a quick check of her hair in the mirror, she left for work.

One of Sara's favorite breakfast foods was a steak and egg bagel, which she regularly stopped for at a little deli half a mile from her apartment. As she pulled into the parking lot, her cell phone rang. "Hello?"

"Miss Eckels? This is Rindy Wallace from the post office."

"Oh, hi. I mean, good morning." Sara replied.

"Miss Eckels, we have a package here with your address on it, but there is no return address. We do not deliver packages without a return address. I'm not sure who dropped it off. Would you like to claim it?"

Sara thought about it for several seconds. *Who would be sending me a package?*

"Umm, I suppose so, Mrs. Wallace. Can I pick it up around 1:00 p.m.?"

"Certainly. Now, the other reason I called is to reply to the message you left for our rural route carrier yesterday."

"Yes, of course," Sara replied. She had called the post office and left her number for Clark Wright, the mailman who delivered the mail to Devil Hollow.

"Well, he will not be in until Saturday. He is semiretired and only works one day a week now."

"I see. Do you have a phone number for him? I couldn't find a listing in the book."

"We do not give out our employee's' phone numbers; however, I can call him and give him yours."

"That would be great! Thank you Mrs. Wallace."

Sara went inside the deli and ordered her bagel. At least she had several things to look forward to today, including a mysterious package and an interview with the mailman who had told Mr. Johnson about the biweekly mail runs from Devil Hollow. Sara was very interested in meeting the old man who Mr. Johnson claimed had met him with the census forms. Perhaps Clark Wright could give her the details on how to accomplish that.

Ned arrived at the bureau parking lot at the same time as Sara Eckels. As she exited her car, Ned quickly noted that she was not wearing a skimpy skirt like she had been the previous day. He actually felt a tinge of disappointment. She was a breath of fresh air in the stuffy, old office building, which was dominated by middle-aged men wearing blue or gray suits. For his part, Ned never wore a suit jacket--- just slacks and a dress shirt with a tie. *I'm a real rebel!* He thought with a smile.

"What's so funny?" Sara asked as she noticed his smile.

"Nothing. Are you going to a funeral today?"

"Why would you ask that?" Sara answered in a surprised tone.

"You're dressed in black slacks and a black blouse, that's why."

Sara smiled. "I'm working on an investigation, Mr. Waters, and it requires that I dress appropriately!"

Ned flashed a smile back at her. "Well, let's hope you clear the case quickly, so you can dress more inappropriately."

Sara started to reply when a dark sedan pulled into the parking lot. A young man wearing black slacks and a white shirt got out of the car and approached Ned and Sara. They both noticed his shoulder holster and gun right away. Ned recognized him as Sergeant Brad Hunt of the city homicide squad. They both worked out at the same gym.

Ned stepped forward and extended his hand toward Hunt. "Brad, how are ya? What brings you to the bureau?"

"Hi Ned. Business, I'm afraid. I need to ask this young lady a few questions."

"What? Me? Wh-why?" Sara stammered.

Sergeant Hunt raised his hand and said "Now, just calm down. It's okay. You're not in any trouble. I just need to ask you a couple of questions."

"What's going on, Brad?" Ned asked.

"We received a coroners call early this morning over at Jim Johnson's place. A neighbor found him dead."

Sara's hand flew up to her mouth "Oh my God!"

"Miss Eckels was seen speaking with the deceased yesterday afternoon," Sergeant Hunt continued. "I already spoke to the taxi driver, Miss Eckels. I just need to know what your business with Mr. Johnson was, and how he seemed to be acting at the time."

Sara began shaking. Ned placed his arm around her shoulder, which gave her some comfort. "My God, he's dead? I was...I was asking him some questions about a census he helped with a few years ago," Sara said as the sobs began to work their way up into her throat.

"Give her a minute, Brad," Ned said. He walked Sara over to the picnic table that sat in front of the office building entryway. Sara sobbed into his shoulder for nearly a minute before finally composing herself. Ned looked at Brad and nodded.

"Miss Eckels...Sara...how was Mr. Johnson acting at that time?" the sergeant asked in a quiet voice.

More employees were arriving in the parking lot and were casting curious looks toward Ned, Sara, and the sergeant.

"He…he was fine. I mean, he seemed okay. He answered my questions and then asked for some money…for beer, I guess. So I gave him ten dollars and left."

"Okay. That goes along with what the taxi driver told us. I'm so very sorry to upset you, Sara, but we need to follow up on all leads when someone dies suddenly. I appreciate your cooperation."

After the sergeant left, Ned walked Sara into the office building lobby. "Look, if you want to take the day off, go ahead," he said softly.

"No, I'll be fine Ned. Thank you. I just need to freshen up my face."

Sara walked into the ladies' room in the lobby and sat her purse beside the sink. She looked into the mirror and saw the dark streaks of mascara dripping down her face. *Good grief, I look like the lead singer for KISS.* She washed her face, opened her purse, and reapplied her makeup. While she had not been there when Mr. Johnson had died, this was as close to death as she had ever come. None of her relatives, other than her stepfather, had died, and he wasn't really what she considered family. To think that she had just been talking to this man less than twenty-four hours ago made the tears begin to well up again.

Ned walked into Mike Evans' office without knocking. He gave Mike a quick briefing of what had just occurred in the parking lot.

"How is she?" Mike asked.

"I think she'll be fine, but it's your call, Mike."

"Let her get cleaned up Ned, then have her come and see me."

"Okay, thanks."

Ned went to his office and turned on the coffeemaker. This was turning out to be an exciting day, at least by bureau standards.

CHAPTER SIX

C lark Wright parked his 1990 Ford F-150 pickup near the old river bridge road and turned off the ignition. The motor sputtered a few times, shaking the entire vehicle before going silent. He had delivered the package for Sara Eckels to the post office before it had opened, and he now awaited further instructions from him. For thirty-five years, Clark had been assigned to the rural postal route that included Devil Hollow. In all those years, he had never crossed over the shallow, quick-flowing rocky stream that had once held the deep waters of the Licking River.

In 1955, the state had torn down the dam that had been located about fifty miles downstream. The river had nearly run dry, and the old bridge had been torn down for safety reasons. A new one had never been built, and no one had ever requested one. The mountain folk of Devil Hollow were essentially stranded. But most said that was the way they preferred it, as many of the people who lived there already had a deep mistrust of the government.

When Clark had been trained by the previous postman who had been responsible for the route, his instructions had been simple; Go to the old river bridge road every other Saturday and wait. A simple pulley system with a large basket and steel cable had been constructed to cross the stream. Clark would place the mail for the residents of Devil Hollow in the basket and pull on the cable until the basket reached the other side. Then he would wait. Usually, within ten minutes or less, a tall dark man would come from behind the tree line across the stream. He would empty the basket, place any outgoing mail inside it, and nod towards Clark. There had been virtually no mail coming from Devil Hollow in the past thirty years, but Clark dutifully included the stop on his route.

This past Saturday, the tall man had placed a package in the basket and attached a note, asking Clark to deliver it anonymously to the post office on Monday, and then return to the old river bridge road on Tuesday. Clark dared not question the odd request. Years before, the tall man had slipped on a rock near the edge of the stream, and his foot had slid into the water. Within seconds, dead fish had begun floating to the surface. Clark had heard tales of evildoing in Devil Hollow, and that moment, so long ago, had sealed it for him. The very fact that no law enforcement or government agency had ever entered the place was another reason. Whatever was going on up there, it was best to ignore it.

As if on cue, the tall man suddenly appeared. He placed a note in the basket and nodded toward Clark, who began pulling on the cable. As the basket reached him, Clark pulled out the note and read it. He looked up and noticed that the tall man was gone. The note said:

Tomorrow two people will come seeking me. You will assist them. Take them upstream to the old Miller farm. There is an old swinging bridge that they can safely cross. You will remember it, as you used to play there as a child.

Clark felt his pulse quicken as he read the last line of the note. *How in the hell could he have known that?* Feeling light-headed, Clark slowly fell to his knees and pulled the handkerchief from his back pocket to dab at the sweat that was rolling down his face. After a few minutes, he stood and slowly walked back to his truck, and then drove to the post office.

As Clark pulled into the loading dock area behind the post office, he saw Rindy Wallace standing by the back door smoking a cigarette.

"Well hello, Clark! Here to pick up your paycheck?"

"Yeah, I reckon so. Ain't much of a check nowadays, but it helps keep a fella fed."

"Why don't you just retire and collect your full pension pay, Clark? Seems like a man your age should be enjoying life."

"I intend to, Rindy...very, very soon," Clark responded as he walked toward the loading dock.

"By the way, some youngster from the Bureau of Statistics called for you. She wanted to ask you some questions about Devil Hollow. I have her number if you want to call her back."

Clark froze in mid stride. His heart rate jumped back up again. He didn't need to ask the name. He knew it would be the name that was on the package he had delivered.

"I believe her name was Sara Eckels," Rindy continued.

CHAPTER SEVEN

Ned paced back and forth in his office as he waited for Sara to come out of the restroom. He was genuinely concerned about her, which surprised him, because he had never had any real feelings for a woman before. One of his greatest insecurities was opening up to a female…or anyone, for that matter. For most of his adult life, women had been merely sex toys to him. It's not that he had planned it that way, but being a star athlete had meant that pretty girls had been ready and willing to sleep with him ever since high school. He'd never had to ask a girl out; they'd just kept coming to him.

Ned had never gotten to know any of them because every time he'd begin dating one, another one would come along to tempt him. He'd never found one whom he felt was more special than the others. Variety was the spice of life, and his future in football had been far more important than any concern about shattering a young girl's heart. He had been encouraged along the way by his teammates, who had kept a running tally of his conquests. The only advice he'd ever received from any adult influence had been from an assistant football coach in high school, who had handed him a brown paper bag full of condoms and said, "You've got a bright future, son. Don't screw it up by knocking up one of those floozies!"

That pattern had continued into college. Everything had come easily to Ned Waters. The women had been constant, and every alumnus and booster had stood in line to tell him how great he was. But when he'd received the knee injury that had ended his football career, everything had changed. Suddenly his close 'friends' had become distant acquaintances before disappearing altogether. They had lost their interest in a has-been. Ned had come to appreciate the true-blue fans in later years. They had been the ones who had continued to invite him to speak at their school banquets, or sign autographs at some charity event.

As for the women... he had continued his conquest mentality. He hadn't known any different, and whenever a woman had shown the slightest interest in a long-term relationship, he had simply dumped her and waited for another. In the last couple of years he had begun to realize that he was growing old, had no kids, and might very well never enjoy the rich benefits of marriage. But this realization may have come too late for Ned. It now gnawed at him some nights, causing him to lose sleep. The one thing he feared most was dying alone.

When Sara finally walked into his office, Ned was still deep in thought.

"A penny for your thoughts, Ned."

Ned jumped at the sound of her voice, nearly knocking over the coffee mug on his desk.

"Sara! How are you feeling?"

"I'm okay. I was just kinda, well...shocked." Sara slumped into the chair across from him.

"Are you sure? Mike wants to talk to you. He wants you to convince him that you're okay."

"I'm a little shaken, Ned, but honestly, I think I'd be better off here at work than at home."

"I'm not the one you have to convince. Let's go see the boss man."

They entered Mike Evans' office and took a seat. Mike studied Sara for a few seconds before he spoke. "How are you, Sara?"

"I'm really okay, Mr. Evans. It's just that…, well, I've never really been around death before. It just freaked me out."

"Sara, we have a very extensive employee benefits package here at the bureau. You are entitled to go home if you wish. I can also offer you counseling services through the company; the first three visits are free."

Sara smiled and looked her boss square in the eyes. "Sir, I know you have to say all of that bull crap. But I'm telling you that I'm fine and wish to continue working."

Ned snickered--a little too loudly--and was the recipient of a glare from Mike Evans. "Sorry, boss," Ned muttered.

"Very well, Miss Eckels. You may return to work. But if at any time you feel the need to leave, you are free to do so."

"Thank you sir, and…" Sara's cell phone rang, and she excused herself. As she walked out of the office to answer it, Mike looked over at Ned. "Could you at least *try* to act like a professional?"

Ned laughed. "Come on, Mike! You should have heard yourself… all serious and shit!"

"Get the hell out of here before I send *you* home!" Mike barked.

Ned returned to his office and found Sara there; she was just hanging up her cell phone. "That was the mail carrier that Mr. Johnson told me about. He said he could meet us tomorrow morning at 9:30 a.m. and show us where he makes his mail deliveries to Devil Hollow."

"My, oh my! You certainly are on top of this case, Watson!" Ned said with a big grin on his face.

"Indeed sire," Sara replied with a terrible English accent as she bowed.

"Well then, the game is afoot!" Ned laughed.

Sara turned to go to her office, and then stopped and turned back toward Ned. "I have to go to the post office on my lunch break to pick up a package. Would you mind going with me? We could pick up some drive-through food on the way."

Ned looked at Sara and smiled. "Sure, but we're not taking that piece of junk that you drive!"

At 12:45 p.m. Ned and Sara pulled out from the parking lot in Ned's shiny red BMW. There was little conversation between them. He pulled his car into the post office lot at 12:58 p.m. "I'll be right back," Sara promised as she hopped out of the car. He watched her as she strolled through the front door. *That girl has some spunk.* In a few minutes, she returned to his car carrying a small manila envelope.

"That's the package?"

"I guess so. I can't wait to see who it's from." She tore the top off the envelope.

As she pulled the contents out of the envelope, Ned put the BMW in reverse and began backing out of the parking spot.

"Oh my God!! Oh please, NO!!! Sara shrieked.

CHAPTER EIGHT

N ed's right foot hit the brake hard, and the engine stalled as his left foot slipped off the clutch. "Sara! What is it?"

Sara sat very still, with a look of sheer terror on her face. Ned restarted the engine and pulled the car into a parking spot. He looked over at Sara, who was shaking, and had lost all the color from her face. He reached over and pulled the type-written, single-sentence note from her hand and read it:

Daddy's home bitch!!!!

Ned had no idea what it meant, or why it had caused such a reaction from Sara. "Sara, please. What can I do? What does this mean?" he asked as he held the note up.

"Ned, can you please drive me somewhere? Anywhere…just drive." Her voice was barely more than a whisper.

"Of course, Sara." He slowly backed the car out of the parking spot and eased onto the highway, heading toward his condo. She sat very still, not speaking or moving. He was beginning to think that she was going into shock. Whatever the words on that note meant to her, it was definitely something evil. He had never seen anyone looking so genuinely terrified.

They arrived at Ned's condo fifteen minutes later. He shut off the motor and walked around to open her door. She sat motionless, staring straight ahead. "Sara? We're at my house. Do you want to come inside? Sara?" She did not respond, and now he was really beginning to think that maybe he should call 911. He started to pull his cell phone from his pocket when she finally spoke "I thought he was dead. All these years, and I thought he was dead." She spoke the words in a monotone, and he knew she was thinking out loud, not actually speaking to him.

He reached down and placed his hand on her shoulder. "Sara! Are you okay?"

She seemed to break out of her daze and she looked up at him. "Yes, I am. How many times are people going to ask me that question today?"

Ned breathed a small sigh of relief. Her spunk was still there, so perhaps the shock was wearing off. "Come on inside Sara. I think you need a drink."

They walked inside and he walked her over to the sofa. "Just have a seat and I'll fix you a stiff drink."

She sat back in the plush sofa and closed her eyes. Within a few minutes, he returned with a glass of whiskey splashed over two cubes of ice. "I watered it down a little. Don't know what kind of tolerance you have for alcohol." He handed her the drink.

"Thanks, Ned." She took the drink.

He sat in the recliner across the room and waited until she had taken a few sips of her drink before he spoke again. "Sara, I have to ask you. What in the hell is going on?"

She took a big drink and sat the glass down on the coffee table. She looked at him, let out a big sigh, and started talking. She told him about her childhood, losing her father at a young age, and then suffering through the mental and sexual abuse at the hands of her stepfather. "After he beat my mom up so badly that she ended up in the hospital, he went to jail. That's when the social services people stepped in and began interviewing me. When the sexual abuse charges were added to his felony assault charges, he was sentenced to prison. Mom and I moved away." Sara stopped talking, took another long drink from the glass, and then continued.

"I went through a lot of therapy, and so did Mom. She actually held some resentment toward me because I never told her what he had done to me. She also felt a lot of guilt because she had brought him into our lives. We were able to work through it though. I heard that he was killed by a drunk driver shortly after he was released from prison. I was so relieved! But now...."

"But now what?" Ned asked. "What does the note have to do with your dead stepfather?"

Sara looked at Ned with a very sad look on her face. "When he would come home drunk in the middle of the night, and sneak into my room, he would always whisper the words you saw on the note. Ned, I never, ever told anyone about that. Ever! The only person who would know it would be..." Her voice trailed off.

"Your stepfather," Ned finished her thought.

"Yes, which means he's still alive. Oh God Ned...what if he's coming for me? What if he

wants to punish me for sending him away?"
She began to shake again, and he immediately
walked over to the sofa and sat down beside
her. Placing his arm around her shoulders, he
pulled her toward him. She buried her face in his
shoulder and began to sob.

After her sobs subsided, he gently slipped his
arm off her shoulder and excused himself. He
walked out onto the patio and pulled out his cell
phone. He called his police buddy, Brad Hunt,
and asked if he could stop by right away. He then
walked back inside and found her standing in
the kitchen. "Can I use your bathroom, Ned?"

"Sure Sara. It's down the hall…first door on
your left."

Ned called the office and spoke to Mike. He
advised him that they had stumbled into another
lead, and would be getting back to the office later
than expected. Sara came out of the bathroom
and walked over to Ned. "Thank you so much
for putting up with me. I know I've been really
unstable the past two days."

"No problem Sara."

"Shouldn't we be getting back to the
office now?"

"Not just yet."

She looked at him quizzically. For a second, she allowed herself to think that he might be suggesting that she stay longer for romantic purposes. Even in her current state of mind, that was a possibility that she actually hoped for. However, he quickly swatted that thought away. "I've asked Sergeant Hunt to stop by, Sara. You need to make a police report."

"Oh…yes, of course. Thank you Ned," she replied, trying very hard to hide her disappointment.

Brad Hunt arrived and Sara went over her story again. Hunt made a phone call and after a few minutes, he received a call back. "Sara, your stepfather is alive. He was released from prison two weeks ago. I strongly recommend that you drive to the magistrate office and get a restraining order against him."

"I'll take you, Sara." Ned said.

Ned thanked Brad for coming over. After the sergeant left, Ned turned to Sara and said, "Let's do this."

CHAPTER NINE

As Ned drove toward town, he glanced over at Sara, who had dozed off. He wasn't surprised, given all that she had been through in the last twenty-four hours. Of course, the whiskey had probably contributed to her condition as well. Ned was beginning to develop feelings for Sara---not sexual feelings, but protective ones. He recognized her beauty, and he certainly appreciated her body, but what he was feeling now was something new to him. He glanced over at her every few minutes as he held the speedometer at a steady 55 mph. The sign ahead read "GROVER MILLS – 8 MILES."

The fact that the Kentucky Bureau of Statistics was located in a small community like Grover Mills was something that had struck Ned as odd when he had arrived there twenty years ago. It hadn't taken long to find out why. In 1985, the year the contract to build the bureau had been awarded to the town, the brother-in-law of the governor also happened to be the mayor of

Grover Mills. The influx of jobs and disposable income had gotten him reelected several times. Before the bureau arrived, Grover Mills had been a dying town.

In the 1920s, outside corporations had begun buying up thousands of acres in the area. Soon the lumberjacks had arrived and had begun cutting down the massive forests in and around Grover Mills. Being in the eastern part of the state, where the mountains were high, the companies had needed a way to get the lumber to the nearby Ohio River. A railway had been suggested, but it would have taken years to complete, and the cost would have been steep. So, they had built a dam fifty miles downstream, which had caused the small Licking River to swell, flooding thousands of acres of farmland. Countless poor Appalachians had been forced out of their homes and off the land that their ancestors had worked and farmed for so many years.

As the river level had swelled and peaked, the loggers had been able to float the timber to the Ohio River, where it had eventually been sold in Cincinnati. The displaced poor had received a stipend from the corporations for their land.

Thanks to large "donations" to the Kentucky elected officials by the big corporations, the stipends had been agreed upon by the State House as "adequate and of fair value." Those not wishing to sell had had no choice. Their land would have been taken by force if necessary.

After the corporations had stripped the thousands and thousands of acres of woodland, they had simply left. Local businesses had begun to close within a year of their departure. Soon, hotels, restaurants, and grocery stores had been shuttered. None of the money from all that timber had gone back into the town or into any part of eastern Kentucky. Instead, it had all gone to the greedy corporations in the north. The hotels, restaurants, and stores had then been owned by the corporations, and the locals who had been lucky enough to be employed had been paid with company script, which could only have been used to purchase items from the corporation-owned businesses. Big money had taken full advantage of the hard-working and honest folk in the Appalachians.

It was ironic that in later years the media would mock the poor people who had been left behind, referring to them as "Hillbillies." But then again, the newspapers had been owned by rich men looking for a story that would sell their papers. Once more, the rich had taken advantage of the Appalachian people.

Ned saw that they were nearly within the city limits. He reached over and gently nudged Sara on the arm. She stirred and slowly opened her eyes.

"Have a nice nap?"

Sara yawned and looked at Ned with a smile. "Thanks for letting me sleep."

"Seemed like the only way to have a peaceful trip," he answered with a wink.

"I'm serious, Ned…Comedy Central. Send in a demo tape," she replied as she slapped his arm.

Ned pulled into the courthouse parking lot. They exited the car and walked over to a side entrance, which was marked with a sign that read "MAGISTRATE OFFICE."

They entered the lobby and walked over to the receptionist desk. The young lady at the desk looked up and said with a smile, "Can I help you?"

Ned explained that they were there to secure a restraining order on the advice of Sergeant Hunt.

After the receptionist wrote down their names, she stood and walked through the door behind her. A few moments later, she emerged and said, "Judge Hicks will see you now."

Judge Hicks, who looked more like Judge Judy of TV fame, sat behind an old oak desk and was peering over her bifocals as they entered. "Have a seat. Sergeant Hunt has already notified me about your situation."

Ned and Sara sat in the two old wooden chairs the judge had indicated.

"I have all the facts I need for probable cause, so I'm granting your request, Miss. Eckels."

"Thank you," Sara said.

"Fill out this affidavit and sign it. I'll also need to see the note you received from the post office," the judge continued in a business-like tone.

"Yes, Ma'am."

Sara took the form and stared at it. She couldn't possibly write all the reasons she was frightened of her stepfather on the small piece of paper that had been handed to her.

Judge Hicks looked at her and said in a softer voice, "Honey, just sign your name. I've read the police report from West Virginia. My secretary can type in the rest."

Sara looked up and gave the judge a grateful smile. "Thank you."

After receiving a copy of the order, Sara and Ned left the magistrate office. "We really need to get back to the office," he said. "I'm pretty sure Mike is wondering what happened to us."

As they walked to the car, she reached over and took hold of his arm. "Ned, I don't know how to thank you. You've been so kind to me. I've never had a man who…well…." Sara's voice trailed off, and she looked towards the ground.

He sensed that she was trying to express her gratitude but didn't know how. He took her hand from his arm and held it gently. "Sara, you're a redneck."

She looked up at his face and burst out laughing. They got into his car and began the short drive back to the office.

CHAPTER TEN

After the past twenty-four hours, Sara just wanted to go home and crawl into bed. She was mentally exhausted. She drove straight home from work, taking care to lock the dead bolt after entering her apartment. The note had reawakened a fear that she had thought had long since passed. Years of therapy had helped her understand that what had happened to her as a child was not her fault. When she had heard that her stepfather had been killed, the relief itself had seemed to act as a healing agent, which had cleansed her soul more than any therapist ever had. Now that she knew he was alive, the bandage had been ripped away, and the old wound was once again bare and bleeding.

Sara had no desire to take her evening bath tonight. She undressed, put on a nightgown, and then walked into the kitchen and poured a small amount of wine into a glass. She opened the cabinet over the stove and pulled out a small bottle. She opened it, shook three of the small tablets into her palm, and then placed them in her mouth. She quickly washed them down with the wine and walked into her bedroom. She seldom took sleeping pills anymore, but she was glad she still had them. All she wanted to do was sleep and awaken to a new day.

After closing her bedroom blinds to block out the summer evening sunshine, she flipped on the small TV on her nightstand and turned the volume down to its lowest level. This had always comforted her; she fell asleep every night with the flickering screen next to her. She pulled her fluffy body pillow close, wrapping an arm and leg over it and pulling it snuggly against her. She closed her eyes and wondered if she would be able to fall asleep, even after taking the sleeping pills. Her breathing slowed, and within a few seconds, she was fast asleep. A few hours later, she began to dream…

Sara was back in West Virginia in her childhood bed. She could hear the TV downstairs as her mother watched the news on the local station in Wheeling. The front door opened and closed, and Sara could hear her mother arguing with her stepfather. There were a few minutes of yelling before things became quiet. Sara heard them go to their bedroom and saw the hall light go out. She knew what was coming next. In an hour, maybe less, her stepfather would sneak into her room. It only happened when he came home late, and Sara prepared herself.

She quietly put on a pair of skintight jeans, making sure they were on backwards to thwart his drunken attempts to undo them. She then pulled a bra from under her bed; it was much too tight for her, so he would be unable to remove it. It only took her a few moments to do this. It was a tried-and-true routine that twelve-year-old Sara had devised to deflect her stepfather's drunken advances. She knew that he would give up quickly, and likely end up pawing at her through her clothing. She had accepted this, although the stench of his breath and the weight of his body on her small frame concerned her more than his hands. Sara was a smart young woman, and she knew that someday his advances might escalate past the pawing. She could not comprehend exactly how, but, instinctually, she knew.

The telltale creaking of the hallway floorboards warned Sara that he was coming. She took a few deep breaths and shut her eyes tight. The bedroom door opened slowly, and Sara could sense the presence of someone in her room. She didn't move. She heard the footsteps as they shuffled over the oak floor toward her bed. She waited for him to whisper those hated words…those three words that struck fear into her heart. She could smell the beer in the air. But the familiar words never came. She heard a voice, but it was not her stepfather's.

Sara sat up and saw Jim Johnson standing at the foot of her bed. He smiled at her, raised a can of Budweiser beer, and then took a swig from it.

"I really appreciate your buying me this beer Sara! I was getting pretty thirsty."

She looked at him, not believing her eyes.

Jim Johnson took another drink and then looked at Sara. "You were kind to me, and I want to return that favor. Don't go into the hollow, Sara."

Sara began to respond, but Jim Johnson cut her off. "Sara, stop fearing the past. It comes with a price. If you keep running up your bill, the Meter Man will collect."

Sara tried to speak, but a loud beeping noise drowned out her voice. The noise got louder and louder as Jim Johnson faded away. BEEP! BEEP! BEEP! BEEP! BEEP! BEEP! She suddenly awoke from her dream as the alarm clock on her nightstand beeped away. She reached over and shut it off, her heart beating loudly in her ears. *What the hell?* She was sweating, and her body pillow was damp from it. She glanced over at the small TV and saw an actor raising a can of Budweiser toward the camera and saying, "This Bud's for you!" Sara let out a small sigh of relief. *It was just a dream!* She laid her head back on the pillow and laughed. Although there was nothing funny about her dream, or about anything else that had happened to her lately, Sara always seemed to manage a laugh even during inappropriate times. Her therapist called it a 'stress-relief valve'.

After switching off the TV, Sara got out of bed and took a quick shower. Despite the dream, she was in good spirits. She was going to spend the morning with Ned Waters while they met with the postal worker, Clark Wright. After she brushed her teeth and put on her makeup, she decided to wear something a little 'special' for Ned today. She had a low-cut blouse that was a little loose on top. She opted to go braless to see if he took notice. She checked herself in the mirror several times before heading out the door for the drive to work. It would be the last time she ever saw her apartment.

CHAPTER ELEVEN

Ned was waiting for Sara in the bureau parking lot. He checked his watch several times. It was unusual for her to be late. When she finally arrived, he walked over to her car and opened the driver side door for her. "About time you got here. Work starts at 9:00 a.m., in case you forgot."

Sara looked up and thought she detected a little annoyance in his tone. "I'm sorry. I took some sleeping pills last night, and I overslept a bit."

Ned's tone softened as he took notice of Sara's blouse when she exited her car. "That's okay. I just don't want to be late meeting Clark Wright. He did say we should be there at 9:30 a.m., and it's a good thirty-minute drive to the old river bridge road."

"I'm ready Ned. Let's go." Sara walked toward his BMW.

"Whoa, girl! We're not taking my baby on that bumpy old road! There's a taxi sitting right over there by the front door." Ned pointed toward the bureau's main entrance.

They both got into the taxi and Ned gave the driver the directions. The driver gave him a questioning look, but said nothing. As they exited the parking lot, Ned rolled down his window. It was a sunny day, but the temperature was still in the sixties. The weather in the mountains could fluctuate as much as forty degrees on a typical summer day. By afternoon, the temperatures would be nearing triple digits. He glanced over at Sara, who was looking out her window at the passing scenery. His eyes drifted from her face down to her chest. The loose-fitting blouse did little to hide her pert breasts, and Ned noticed immediately that she was not wearing a bra. He stared for a few seconds before turning his head and looking out the window.

Sara smiled. She had not rolled down her window, and could see Ned's reflection in the glass as she pretended to be admiring the passing landscape. He was looking at her, and she was pretty sure the blouse was having its desired effect. She could feel the wind blowing through the taxi from Ned's open window, and it was tugging at her blouse in such a way as to make it fall open. She had also noticed Ned taking a quick peek at her cleavage when she had climbed from her car earlier. She decided that a combination wardrobe of the pleated skirt from Monday and this blouse might just drive him crazy.

The taxi slowed, took a turn, and left the main road. The next five miles were spent bumping along on old Route 22. Although it had once been paved, the big logging trucks that had rumbled along it decades ago had reduced it to rubble and ruts. They finally arrived at the intersection of the old river bridge road, where Ned saw Clark's aging, beat-up Ford pickup waiting for them near the river. The taxi slowed to a stop and the driver turned to Ned. "Do you want me to wait for you?"

"Yeah, this won't take long," Ned replied.

He and Sara got out of the taxi and walked over to the pickup truck. Clark was sitting inside, smoking a cigar. Ned walked up to the driver door and introduced himself. Clark nodded at him, and climbed from the truck. Sara walked over and Ned said "And this is---"

"Sara Eckels," Clark interrupted. "Pleased to meet you both."

Sara shook Clark's hand and said, "Well, let's get right to it. I don't want to take up too much of your time, Mr. Wright."

She explained that they were investigating the odd census numbers that had been returned from the residents of Devil Hollow. She told him about Jim Johnson and asked if Clark remembered him.

"I sure do, young lady. Nice fella! I've been meeting census takers out here every ten years since I began this route. They deliver the census forms just like I deliver the mail...by the pulley basket." Clark pointed toward the cable and basket that spanned the Licking River.

Ned looked at Clark in disbelief. "You're telling me that in this day and age, the only way to get mail in and out of Devil Hollow is by this method?"

Clark studied Ned for a moment, and continued, "The folks up there in Devil Hollow are a reclusive lot, and we respect that. Every man has a right to his way of living. Don't you agree, Mr. Waters?"

Ned heard the sarcasm in Clark's voice, and decided to keep his mouth shut and allow Sara to do the talking.

Sara sensed it too, and quickly asked, "So can we meet the man who you deliver and collect the mail from? Mr. Johnson said you arranged for him to get the census forms in and out of Devil Hollow, and this man met him here."

Clark smiled. "I've already made arrangements for you to meet him. There's an old swinging bridge about one mile upstream from here. He will be there at 10:00 a.m. We really need to get started if we want to arrive on time."

Sara smiled and took Ned's hand in hers, "Come on Sherlock, the game is afoot!"

Ned hesitated before walking with Sara as they followed the old mailman along the side of the river and into the woods. There was something about the way that Clark Wright smiled that made the hair on the back of his neck stand up. He had seen that smile before from certain boosters who had assured him that he would always be a part of the Kentucky Wildcat football family. It was thick with fakeness.

They walked along a path that seemed impossibly perfect for this area. Clark was nimble and spry for his age, and Ned found himself straining to keep up with him. Although the underbrush was thick around them, the path was clear and smooth. They arrived at the bridge after a twenty-minute hike. It looked ancient, but solid. The wooden planks were moss covered, yet the thick ropes that supported them appeared stable. Clark stopped and pointed across the river. There, on the other side, stood a tall dark figure. The figure raised his hand in greeting, and Clark waved back.

"So, what do we do now?" Ned asked.

"We go talk to him!" Sara responded as she pulled Ned onto the bridge.

They slowly edged their way across the bridge, which swayed slightly with each one of their steps. Ned glanced back at Clark, who gave him a wave and another one of those thick, fake smiles. Ned stopped. "Sara, I don't have a good feeling about this." She looked back at him and laughed. "Come on, Ned! Don't be such a chicken! The bridge will hold us!" Ned slowly crept forward, holding onto Sara's hand.

Clark watched them and felt a sadness enveloping his soul. He could still see them, but it was like looking at someone through a pane of frosty glass. The window to this world had closed on them the moment they'd stepped on that bridge. It would never open again. They

belonged to the Meter Man now. Clark walked
back down the path until he reached the road.
He pulled a fifty dollar bill from his wallet and
handed it to the taxi driver. "They decided to go
exploring," Clark told the driver. "You can go."

CHAPTER TWELVE

Ned felt a little nauseous as they neared the middle of the bridge. He was never fond of heights, and, at that moment was looking down through a hole in the wooden planks at a thirty-foot drop to the rocky rapids below. Sara felt his hand squeezing hers a little more tightly. She turned and saw that he was looking rather pale in the face. She coaxed him along in a cheerful voice, "Come on, tough guy. Almost there!"

Ned knew that looking down wasn't a good idea, but neither was having his foot fall through the aging timber. He kept one hand on the rope railing and held onto Sara's hand with the other. It wasn't so much the creaking wood as it was the constant swaying that caused him to feel ill. The humidity in the woods was heavy as the temperature began to rise. He felt the sweat dripping from his forehead and running in little streams down his neck---no doubt as much a result of his nightly drinking as it was the heat.

Sara looked toward the tall man at the end of the bridge and could make out his facial features now. He appeared to be older--- perhaps in his early sixties. *Definitely over fifty-five!* She thought. He smiled as he caught Sara looking at him. It was a warm smile that made her feel instantly at ease. The man was wearing dark blue work trousers and a matching button-down shirt. The condition of the bridge improved as they neared the clearing where the man stood waiting, and Ned sighed with relief when they at last stepped off onto solid ground.

"Welcome! My name is Michael," the tall man said as he stepped forward with his hand extended. Ned shook his hand, introducing Sara, and then himself. Ned noticed the same thing Sara had earlier---that the man appeared to be older than fifty-five. Ned thought he bore a striking resemblance to the actor who had starred in the movie *Silence of the Lambs. What was his name? Anthony Hopkins?*

"Sara and I work for the Kentucky Bureau of Statistics, Michael. We wanted to speak to you about the census reports that were delivered two years ago by a man named Jim Johnson. There seems to be a problem with the data that was collected."

"I see." Michael answered with a smile. "What is it that you find troubling with the data?"

Sara jumped in before Ned could respond, "It's the maximum age of the residents in Devil Hollow. According to the census reports we received, no one there is over the age of fifty-five."

Michael continued to smile, not reacting to Sara's comment. "I've been told that the two of you wish to conduct an investigation into this matter?"

Ned nodded and said, "Yes, that's why we're here, Michael. We were hoping you could clear this up. It's important to have accurate information for our database."

Michael's smile waned ever so slightly, but it was enough for Ned to notice.

"There aren't many of us in Devil Hollow, Mr. Waters. Is this information you seek really going to make a huge difference to your database?"

"Maybe not a huge difference, but it is something we take very seriously. Gathering accurate population numbers, ages, and other information is our job, and we try to do that job to the best of our abilities," Ned answered.

"Of course, Mr. Waters. I wasn't questioning the importance of your job. If the numbers mean that much to you, I can provide them," Michael answered. "We can clear this up right away. We have all the birth records at our community hall. It is only a short walk from here."

Ned looked at Sara, who nodded. "Alright then, let's do this," Ned said.

Michael led the way. The path looked like an old logging road, with some deep ruts from horse-drawn wagons still evident. The trees were not as thick on this side of the river, which was most likely because they were relatively new, replacing the ones that had been cut down for timber. Logging roads were not really 'roads', but more like paths carved into the hillside. Some still served as shortcuts through the woods, but none would ever be able to bear an automobile.

Ned was wondering how long it would be before they reached this community hall Michael had mentioned. Between the one-mile hike to the swinging bridge, and now this little walk, he knew his damaged knee would soon be howling in pain. He noted that Michael was moving at a pretty rapid pace for a man his age. *Must be nice to have two good knees!* He thought to himself. As if sensing Ned's thoughts, Michael turned around and said, "Only a few more minutes and we will reach the village."

Ned tried to keep his prejudiced thoughts in check. He had seen photographs of Appalachian mountain folk who lived in these hollows. They were a rough-looking bunch, sitting on their porches with shotguns cradled in their arms. Ned hoped that this would not be the case today. His thoughts were broken by Sara asking their escort, "So, Michael, not to be impolite, but how old are you?"

"Younger than the mountains, but older than the trees," Michael replied.

Sara laughed loudly as they continued walking along the path. Ned, however, did not laugh. He did not think Michael was funny. There was something about the constant smile on his face that made Ned shiver, even in this heat.

CHAPTER THIRTEEN

The trio rounded a curve in the path, and Ned stopped dead in his tracks. Before him was the village of Devil Hollow. Ned was shocked to see a picture-perfect, Norman Rockwell postcard of a town. To his right were a general store, a schoolhouse, a church, and what appeared to be the community hall. Each of the buildings was painted white. In front of these buildings was a small creek, which was spanned by a wide wooden plank bridge.

To the left of the bridge, Ned could see three rows of well-built houses and cabins, each row separated by streets paved with stones. The homes were small, but very well constructed. They were also painted white, except for the cabins, which were made from logs and bore no paint. The small creek seemed to serve as a dividing line between the residences and the other buildings. The hillside had just enough rise and slope to keep the structures safe from the creek should it ever flood its small banks.

Sara walked over to Ned and whispered, "It's so beautiful."

Michael reached into his shirt and pulled out a gold colored pocket watch. He flipped it open, frowned, and placed it back into his shirt. "We will not be able to search the birth records just yet. It's nearly time for the schoolchildren's lunch recess."

Ned asked, "What does that have to do with checking the birth records?"

Michael smiled. "I apologize; I didn't explain enough. The children use the community hall as a lunch room. It will be much too loud and busy in there."

"Well, I could go for a soda pop," Sara piped in. "Maybe we could buy one at the store while we wait, Ned."

"Sounds good to me!" Ned replied. The long hike, and the heat, had given him quite a thirst. "What do ya say, Michael? Care to join us for a cold one?"

Michael turned to Ned with a quizzical expression on his face. "Cold one?"

"Yeah, you know…a drink?" Ned answered.

"Oh, yes. You will find food and drink within the village store. Take what you like. I need to assist the cooks with the children's lunches. I will join you after they've eaten."

Ned and Sara walked toward the store. "It's no wonder they don't want to be connected to civilization," she mused. "This is heaven."

They entered the store, which was dark inside. "Hello?" Ned called out. No one answered, so he looked around for a light switch. He found it and switched it on. A few small lightbulbs hanging from wires attached to the high ceiling flickered to life. They did little to brighten the dark store.

"TURN IT OFF!"

Ned and Sara both jumped as the voice boomed from across the room.

"I said TURN IT OFF! NOW!!" The voice rose in volume, and in anger.

Ned fumbled for the switch and turned the lights off. There was deathly silence for a few moments, and then they both saw the old man shuffling across the store through the shadows. He passed right by them without a word and threw open the large blinds that covered the front windows. "Devil juice!" the old man hissed.

Sara was clinging to Ned, her fingers digging so hard into his arm that he let out a small yelp of pain. "Damn, girl! Easy!"

The old man stared at them, and Ned saw the anger dissolve quickly from his face. "You are strangers? I'm sorry. You couldn't have known."

"Known what?" Ned asked, feeling a little pissed off. "We came in here for a drink, not to get yelled at!"

The old man took a few steps toward Ned. "I'm sorry. Truly, I am."

Ned calmed down. The old man's tone sounded truly apologetic. "It's okay, Mister. We didn't mean any harm."

The old man stood in front of Ned and Sara with his head bowed as the bright rays of sunshine splashed over the store. Ned felt bad, as he could now see that the old man was bent over with age. He was dressed in the same type of clothing as Michael.

"Help yourselves. There is plenty of food and water," The old man said.

Ned turned and got his first look at the inside of the store. There were no canned goods, candy, or beer coolers. There were only wooden bins along each side of the aisle, and they were overflowing with ears of corn, potatoes, cabbage, and fresh fruits of all sorts. On the bare walls above the bins were metal hooks with chunks of cured meat hanging from them; there was deer, ham, rabbit, and squirrel. Next to the meats were rows of chicken eggs. Ned felt like he was at the farmer's market in Lexington.

Then Ned saw the pump. Right in the middle of the aisle was an aging hand pump with its pipe rising through a hole cut in the wooden floor. Next to the pump was a small metal stand with cups hanging from it. A handwritten sign proclaimed "FREE WATER". Ned turned and saw Sara looking at him. She shrugged her shoulders, walked past him, picked up a cup, and began cranking the old handle on the pump. The water came out slowly but in a steady stream. Ned grabbed a cup and placed it under Sara's. When hers was filled, he filled his.

They both drank deeply, and Ned thought it was the best water he'd ever tasted in his life. It was cool, clear, and refreshing. He pumped out two more cups before his thirst was finally quenched. Sara had already placed her cup back on the stand and was eating some of the grapes and blueberries from the fruit bins. "Ned! You have got to try these!"

They moved among the bins, tasting and sampling. Everything seemed to be delicious.

Ned could not recall any produce he had ever purchased at a farmers market tasting this good. Once they had gotten their fill, Ned walked back toward the front of the store. He glanced around, but didn't see a cash register. The old man was still standing near the front windows, and was now looking outside. Ned walked up behind him and asked, "So what do we owe you?"

The old man turned around, and Ned took a step back when he saw his face. One of his eyes was missing. There was a deep, dark hole where his eye had once been, and there was some kind of oozing gray liquid trickling down over his cheek. "The price has already been paid," the old man said.

"My God! Your eye! Wh-what happened to your eye?"

"He collected. I had no credit left, and when you turned on the electric, he came to seek payment." The old man took a step back and fell against the window. He slowly slid down onto the ground, and his body went limp.

Ned kneeled down and felt the old man's neck. There was no pulse.

CHAPTER FOURTEEN

The door to the schoolhouse burst open, and the giggling students ran or skipped over to the community hall for lunch. Michael was standing there, holding the door open for them. They immediately calmed down when they saw him, and they filed past him quietly. After the last student had entered, he shut the door behind them. As Michael walked toward the store he heard Sara's muffled scream from inside as he neared the front entrance. As he stepped inside, he saw the old man slumped over on the floor, with Ned kneeling beside him and Sara standing over them both with her trembling hand covering her mouth.

"What has happened here?" Michael asked.

Ned looked up and was shocked to see that Michael still had that same big smile on his face. "Someone attacked this old man! They gouged out his eye and killed him!" Ned shouted.

"That is most un-fortunate. He was a good storekeeper," Michael replied.

Ned couldn't understand how Michael could be so calm. Not only was he calm, he was smiling…and there was something else too. Ned could swear that Michael looked ten years younger. *Must be the light in here.*

"His name was Justin Wetzel. He came to us ten years ago. He is not a native of our village," Michael said as he looked down at the body.

"I don't need his life story!" Ned said angrily. "Right now we need to worry about finding the man who killed him!"

Michael ignored Ned's statement and walked outside onto the porch. He picked up a small hammer and struck the bell that was mounted on the wall just outside the doorway. He struck it twice and, almost immediately, two young men came running out of the community hall and over to the store. "Mr. Wetzel has passed on. Please take him to the church and place his body on the altar. I shall tend to him later this afternoon," Michael instructed them.

The young men went inside and carried the frail body of Justin Wetzel from the store. Ned stood up and whispered to Sara, "This guy is nuts! Someone murders this man, and he acts like it's no big deal."

From the front porch, Michael spoke, "Murder is a strong word, Mr. Waters. However, there has been no crime committed here today."

Sara looked at Ned with fear in her eyes. How had Michael heard Ned? Ned walked out onto the porch and said, "Look, whatever just happened to that old man was definitely a crime! How can you possibly stand here and say it isn't?"

Michael looked at Ned, still smiling. "Mr. Wetzel paid for what he used. That is the law here. You will come to understand in time."

Ned was about to speak when the door to the community hall opened. Michael pulled his pocket watch out and looked at it. "Ah, lunchtime is over! It is time for the children to play."

The students ran out into the stone-lined street, where they began playing. Some played tag, some hopscotch, and several jumped rope. Ned stood on the porch, looking over at them with a stunned expression on his face. Sara walked over to Ned and said "My God, Ned. They…they…"

"I know, Sara. I can see."

What Ned and Sara saw were a group of schoolchildren who all appeared, at least physically, to be in their twenties. Ned was scared. He was through with this crazy little town. "Come on, Sara. Screw the birth records! We're leaving."

Michael stood on the porch, right beside them, watching the students play. If he had heard what Ned had said, he had chosen to ignore it. Ned grabbed Sara's hand, and they began walking toward the path that had brought them into Devil Hollow. As they started up the hillside, Ned heard Michael clapping his hands and yelling, "Time to return to your studies children!"

Ned turned and looked back to see Michael staring at his pocket watch. He hoped to never see that madman again. They walked at a brisk pace and were soon deep into the woods and on their way back to the river. Sara had a hard time keeping up. Although she was half Ned's age, he was still bigger and stronger. "Ned, please...I need to rest," she pleaded.

Ned was feeling a little better now that they had put some distance between themselves and the village. "Okay, Sara. Let's take a breather."

They sat quietly for a few minutes. The heat was unbearable, and Ned took his shirt off. It was completely soaked with sweat. Sara looked at his bare chest and thought of the irony. Here she was, in the middle of the woods with the man she longed for, and he was half naked. But she knew nothing was going to happen---not here on this old logging road. As much as she wanted him, getting the hell out of these woods was far more important.

"Sara, we need to talk. Before we get back, we need to decide what to say about the things we saw today."

"I know, Ned. My God, that poor old man! But we didn't really see anyone kill him, right?"

"No, but does that mean we shouldn't report it to the police?"

She stared at the ground. "Of course not, but..."

He sensed that she wanted to forget everything just as much as he did. "Let's just go back to my place, get a shower, and talk about it. We don't have to make a decision right now."

They got back on their feet and began walking. They walked for what seemed like hours. Ned looked around for anything that might look familiar, but the trees and bushes all looked the same. His knee began to ache, and the pain intensified slowly with each step. They took another break and then another. The sky began to darken and he realized that they were lost. He was about to inform Sara that they might need to find a spot to camp for the night when he saw the lights ahead through the trees. She saw them too, and they both hurried ahead.

They rounded a turn on the path, and there stood Michael. "Ah, there you are! It is nearly time to retire for the night," Michael said with a smile as he closed the pocket watch and placed it back into his shirt.

"Come along. I will show you to your homes."

CHAPTER FIFTEEN

S ara fell to the ground and began sobbing. She was completely worn-out from walking for hours, and now they found themselves right back where they had started. Ned stared at Michael with a look of contempt. "Why don't you just direct us back to the swinging bridge? We'll pass on spending the night."

"Do not be so unreasonable, Mr. Waters. It is late, and the woods are not a safe place to be after sunset. We already have comfortable accommodations prepared for both of you."

"What made you so sure we'd be back?" Ned asked.

"We prepared your homes before your arrival, Mr. Waters. There is no return path for you. This is your home now."

Ned looked at Michael and snorted. "Dude, you just got on my last nerve! I've had it with your stupid smile and your stupid village!" Ned took a step toward Michael and drew back his fist. Michael did not move.

"How's that knee feeling Mr. Waters?" Michael asked in a low, hissing voice.

Ned felt the pain immediately. It shot up through his leg like a red-hot poker. He grabbed his knee and fell to the ground beside Sara. Ned felt as if he might pass out, and then the pain slowly eased.

"When you two are ready, you will find a young man waiting for you by the stream. He will show you to your homes. I have other business to attend to now." Michael turned and strolled off toward the village.

Sara looked at Ned, her cheeks still wet with tears. "What are we going to do? I'm scared, Ned!"

Ned rubbed his throbbing knee and watched Michael walking away. He briefly considered going back on the logging road path, but he knew that it would simply lead them in circles. They were both exhausted and needed to rest. "We'll play along for now, Sara. But come sunup, we'll find a way out of here."

They both stood and slowly walked down to the bridge by the stream, where a young man was waiting for them. Without speaking, he turned and walked up the slope toward the houses, motioning for them to follow. They passed by the first row of houses and then the second. The next row was all log cabins, and this was where the man turned and began leading them down the stone-covered street. When they arrived at the penultimate cabin, the man stopped. There was an old woman sitting in a rocking chair on the porch. The man pointed at Sara and then at the old woman. "Here," he said.

Sara looked at Ned, who gave her a hug and said, "It's okay. It's just for the night. You'll be fine!"

The old woman rose from her chair and greeted Sara. "Come along, child. Your bed is prepared."

The young man took a few steps toward the last cabin on the street and pointed at Ned. "Yeah, I know...here!" Ned said sarcastically.

Ned walked up the wooden steps and entered the cabin. It was sparsely furnished, with a large table and two chairs near the fireplace, and two small beds on the far side of the room. There were no rugs, no sink, and no windows. The only light was provided by two candles burning on the mantel. Ned noticed that one of the beds appeared to be occupied. The covers moved, and a voice called out, "Hello? Who is there?"

"Your new roomie!" Ned replied dryly.

The man sat up in the bed. He looked to be ninety years old if he were a day. He gazed at Ned with sadness on his face. "You're a new one. Well, I suppose this is it for me then." The man sighed and lay back down on the bed.

"What in the hell is this place?" Ned said angrily. "What are you talking about?"

The man slowly sat back up in the bed and looked at Ned. "In case you haven't figured it out yet, you're in Hell."

The man climbed from the bed and shuffled over to the table by the fireplace where he eased himself into one of the chairs. He pointed at the other chair, and Ned walked over and sat in it. "Where are you from?" he asked Ned.

"Owensboro."

"Kentucky?"

"Yes. And you?"

"Asheville, North Carolina. What about the girl?"

Surprised, Ned looked up at him. "How did you know I was with a girl?"

The man chuckled and replied, "Because we all came here with a girl! That's how it works."

"How what works? I don't understand what you're saying. Does everyone here talk in riddles?"

The man reached out and took Ned's hand. "Hear my words and listen well! I came here ten years ago with my daughter. We were lured to this place under false pretenses. Once we were here, we couldn't leave. I was brought here to this cabin, just like you were tonight. There was another man here then, and I took his place. You'll be taking mine."

"Why will I be taking your place? I don't understand!"

"Because I can no longer pay for what I use. Everything here is measured. Each drop of water, every morsel of food, and every watt of electricity. I was too ignorant to realize it…until the Meter Man came to collect his first bill."

Ned felt a shudder run down his spine. The old man at the store had said something about not having any credit left, and someone coming to collect…right before he died.

"I know this sounds crazy, but I'm perfectly sane," the man whispered. He let go of Ned's hand and lowered his head.

The room was silent for a few minutes before the man spoke again. "How old do I look?"

Ned stared at the floor. He wasn't sure what to say. This whole day was just a nightmare on steroids to him. Finally, Ned answered, "Ninety? Ninety-five?"

The man sighed as he raised his head and whispered, "I am fifty-one years old."

CHAPTER SIXTEEN

Sara found herself in a cabin identical to Ned's. The old woman pointed toward a small bed in the corner. "That is your bed for tonight. After I am gone, you may take mine."

Sara looked at the woman and asked, "What do you mean, 'after you're gone'? Are you leaving me here alone?"

The woman let out a low, sad laugh. "Not tonight, but soon. You will replace me soon."

"Replace you? I don't understand."

The woman walked over to the fireplace and took a flickering candle from the mantel. She then picked up a new candle and placed its wick under the flame of the lit one. "When things run down, they must be replaced. A candle can only burn for so long," she said as she placed the newly lit candle on the table in front of Sara. "Do you understand that?"

Sara nodded.

"Good. Then simply think of me as the old candle and yourself as the new one. You were brought here because you are young, and new. I am old, and my flame is nearly spent."

"I don't intend to stay here!" Sara said angrily. "This place is crazy, and so are you! First thing in the morning, Ned and I are outta here!"

"Ned? Is he your father?"

Sara blushed. "No, he's my...well, he's my coworker."

"But you're very fond of him, aren't you?"

"That's none of your business lady!"

The woman chuckled sadly and sat down in one of the wooden chairs by the table. "It doesn't matter to me child. You see, I already know that you love him. That is how the Meter Man gets us here."

Sara cringed when the old woman said Meter Man. It was the same name Jim Johnson had mentioned in her dream. "Okay, that's enough!" Sara shouted. "I'm tired, and I need a bath. Just show me where the bathroom is, and after I clean up, I'm going to sleep. I'm not going to deal with this crap anymore!"

The woman pointed to a door behind Sara. "You may bathe in there."

Sara stood up and hurried into the bathroom. She found the light switch, flipped it on, and closed the door behind her. The tiny bathroom was primitive; it had a wooden box in the corner with a hole cut into the top of it. Sara assumed that was the toilet. The bath 'tub' was just that---a large steel tub that sat in the middle of the room. There were no faucets. She sat down on the floor and began sobbing. After a few minutes, there was a light knock on the door. "WHAT?" Sara yelled.

The door creaked open and the old woman said softly, "If you will help me, we can haul in some water from the rain barrel outside. Twenty buckets will provide you with a decent bath."

After ten minutes of alternating trips outside to the rain barrel, the two women managed to fill the steel tub halfway. The old woman handed Sara a bar of lye soap and a soft, old towel. "I'll leave this last bucketful so you can rinse," the old woman said as she sat the wooden bucket on the floor.

"Thank you," Sara said in a softened tone.

After closing the bathroom door, Sara removed her clothing and slid into the tub. The water was cool and was a welcome relief from the heat. After cleaning herself off, Sara stood up and rinsed off her body before wrapping the towel around her. She looked down at her dirty clothes on the floor and decided against putting them back on. She opened the bathroom door and walked back out into the main room of the cabin.

The old woman was sitting at the table with her head lowered in what Sara took as silent prayer. After a few seconds, she raised her head and asked Sara to sit down. "Child, my thoughts were only of myself when you were brought here tonight. I am very sorry. I know you have questions. You may now ask them."

Sara felt bad for raising her voice at the woman earlier. "You said I was brought here to replace you. Please tell me exactly what you meant."

The old woman looked at Sara with eyes that appeared much younger than her withered face. It was probably not something a man would notice, but, to Sara, it was a striking contrast.

The old woman began to speak, and as she told her story, her eyes shone more brightly with each word. "I was fresh out of high school and living with my father in Asheville, North Carolina. I had become engaged at the age of seventeen. My fiancé was an athletic, adventurous man of twenty-two. We intended to get married that autumn, when the leaves were changing colors in the mountains. Two weeks before our wedding, my fiancé left for a hike on the Appalachian Trail. He never returned. After a week of searching, the authorities stopped looking. I never gave up hope, but as October became November, I began to realize that maybe he was gone forever."

The old woman stopped talking and seemed to be struggling to continue. Sara reached across the table, took her hand, and squeezed it. The woman smiled slightly before continuing, "Then, one day, an envelope showed up at our door. Inside was a letter from my fiancé saying he was alive! He had been injured in a fall, but was healing well. Some local villagers in a place called Devil Hollow had found him, and he asked me to come pick him up. Can you imagine my happiness? Father and I raced down here and were led to the old swinging bridge, where we met Michael."

The old woman stopped talking, and her eyes began to darken. Sara urged her to continue.

"Michael led us to Devil Hollow. My fiancé was nowhere to be seen. It did not take us long to figure out that my fiancé had never been here.

We tried to leave, to go back, but…" her voice trailed off, and she once again became silent.

"But you couldn't leave, because the trail led you back to Devil Hollow," Sara said as she finished the old woman's sentence.

"Yes. I was brought to this cabin. There was an elderly woman here, or so I thought."

"What do you mean?" Sara asked.

"Sara, although I may appear very old to you, I am only twenty-eight."

Sara felt faint. The room seemed to spin for a moment, and she grabbed hold of the corner of the table to balance herself. After a few minutes of silence, Sara spoke, "So I'm just going to live in this cabin, get old, and be replaced by a younger girl? Is that what you're telling me? 'Cause that is crazy!"

The old woman looked at Sara, and as the last bit of light in her eyes died out, she replied, "Yes…after you breed, of course."

CHAPTER SEVENTEEN

The first light of dawn filtered through the small cracks in the cabin's walls, causing Ned to slowly open his eyes. It took his mind a moment to adjust to his surroundings, and then his eyes flew open and he sat up with a start. The old man's bed was empty, and he was not in the cabin. However, there was fresh fruit and bread on the table. Ned felt his stomach cramping with hunger, so he helped himself to the food. As he swallowed the last piece of bread, the old man walked in. "You are requested to report to the general store. Michael said to wait there for him," the old man said.

"What if I don't want to?" Ned replied.

"I would not disobey him if I were you," the old man warned. "Not unless you wish to make a payment now."

"Make a payment for what?" Ned asked.

The old man turned and walked outside. Ned followed him onto the porch. Below them, Michael stood in the doorway of the church, looking at his pocket watch. "For your own sake, please go to the store," the old man said in a low voice.

Ned shrugged and started walking down the street toward the store. He would play along until he got a chance to talk with Sara and find a way out of Devil Hollow. If Michael tried to stop them from leaving, Ned intended to use force. He seriously doubted that he would have any problem overpowering Michael. As a matter of fact, he actually wished Michael would try to stop them. If his knee hadn't given out on him last night, he would have decked Michael. *I'd like to give that bastard a shot in the chops,* he thought as his hand curled into a fist. Ned reached the front porch of the store and had a seat on the small wooden bench.

About fifteen minutes later, Michael emerged from the church and walked over to Ned. "I sense your anger, Mr. Waters. I understand it. The others all acted in the same manner. Given time, you will adjust."

Ned felt the strong urge to punch Michael right in the mouth. In fact, he decided that was exactly what he was going to do! As he started to stand up and draw back his fist, Michael flipped

open his pocket watch. Ned felt a searing pain
shooting from his knee. It felt like a hot knife
had been inserted into it and was being rotated.
Ned screamed in agony and fell to the ground.
The pain slowly waned, and he blinked away the
tears as he looked up at Michael.

Michael smiled and closed the pocket watch.
"Shall we get on with our business, Mr. Waters?
Each morning at dawn, you will report here.
You will ring the store bell two times at 6:15 a.m.
Then, at 6:30 a.m., you will ring it three times.
The two rings are to alert the workers that it
is time for them to report to the fields for their
chores. The three rings are to alert the children
to prepare for school. Do you follow me so far?"

Ned pulled himself up onto the bench with
great effort. He started to tell Michael what to
do with his damn bell, but he noticed the pocket
watch and decided to remain silent. He simply
nodded.

"Excellent! It is now 6:15, Mr. Waters," Michael
said as he handed Ned the small hammer he had
used the day before to ring the bell.

Ned took the hammer and struck the bell
twice. A few seconds later, half the front doors to
the houses and cabins opened at nearly the same

instant. Ned stared in disbelief as about fifty men trudged out of the doorways and marched together up a path toward the top of the hill. They were all dressed in blue work pants and shirts similar to Michael's. They all appeared to be very, very old.

"Some of them tend to the gardens on the top of the hill, Mr. Waters. Others take care of the livestock. They each have their duty, just as you do. You were fortunate to arrive when the storekeeper position became available. You will find that it is a much less taxing vocation."

"Michael, look…I don't know if you can understand where I'm coming from, but you can't just keep me here against my will. I really want to go home."

"Mr. Waters, you came here of your own free will. This is your home now."

Michael flipped open the pocket watch and Ned flinched. "It is now 6:30, Mr. Waters."

Ned raised the hammer and struck the bell three times.

The front doors of about twenty-five homes opened and men and women began to spill out onto the streets. Although they all looked to be in their early twenties, they acted like children, skipping, squealing and laughing as they made their way down toward the school. Michael walked to the bridge and gave each of them a hug and kiss as they crossed over it. He then raised his hands, and they all became quiet. "My children, before you begin your studies today, I have a surprise for you. Inside the church is a special treat from your father!"

The students let out a roar of happiness and raced toward the church. After they had all gone inside, Michael stood outside looking intently at his pocket watch. Ned sat down on the wooden bench and rubbed his knee. There was no sign of soreness. Whatever Michael had done to him had now gone. He closed his eyes and leaned his head back against the outer wall of the store. It was getting hot already.

The front door of the church flew open, and the sound of the students' laughter brought Ned out of his daze. He opened his eyes and saw the small figures running past him toward the schoolhouse. A young boy, perhaps ten years old, brushed by Ned, tapping him on the arm as he passed by, saying "Tag, you're it!"

Ned looked down at his sleeve where the little boy had touched him and saw blood.

CHAPTER EIGHTEEN

The ringing of the store bell startled Sara out of a restless sleep. She had not slept well, especially after the old woman had made the comment about breeding. Sara had pressed her for details, but the woman had ignored her, walking over to her bed and falling asleep. Although her mind had been racing with questions, Sara had eventually dozed off, exhausted from the events of the day. She wrapped the sheet around her as she stood, looking over at the old woman's bed, which was empty. She walked into the bathroom and saw that her clothes were no longer on the floor. *Great! What am I supposed to wear?*

The front door opened, and the old woman walked in carrying a basket of fruits in one hand and a bundle of clothing in the other. She placed the basket on the table and the clothing on Sara's bed. "Eat, child, then get dressed. We will be taking lunch to the men in the fields later, and we must begin preparing it now."

"Lunch to the men? I don't follow what you're saying."

"We each have a job to do, and yours has been selected. As my replacement, you need to learn mine," the old woman said in a matter-of-fact tone.

"Okay lady, listen up. I'm tired of the games! What in the hell is going on around here?" Sara shouted in anger.

The woman looked at her sadly. "When I told you my story last night, I thought you understood. You were brought here to take my place. You will do the same tasks I have performed. That's all there is to it."

"I do not want to take your place, and no one can force me to!"

"Child, you can yell and scream and even throw a tantrum if you wish, but what's done is done. You cannot leave this place...ever."

Sara walked over to the basket of fruits on the table and selected an apple, which she promptly hurled against the fireplace. "Tantrum? You wanna see a tantrum? I'll show you a---."

Sara's next words froze in her mouth as the tall shadow fell across the doorstep. She turned toward the door and saw Michael standing there.

He glared at her, unsmiling, with eyes that were black. Slowly, he raised his pocket watch and flipped it open.

Sara felt a rush of wind blow by her face. The cabin began to spin, and she staggered, falling to the floor. The room grew darker, and then she passed out.

Sara began to dream, and found herself in her childhood bedroom. She was naked. The creaking of the floorboards sent chills throughout her tiny, young body. She tried to move, to cover herself, but could not. Her bedroom door opened, and there stood her drunken stepfather. "Daddy's home, bitch!" he said with a grin as he stumbled toward her bed.

Sara screamed, but no sound came from her throat. He came closer and was now sitting next to her on the bed. She could smell the liquor, and she could see the lust in his eyes as they pored over her nakedness. "This won't hurt much, little girl. Just make sure you keep quiet!"

Sara woke up on the floor of the cabin screaming, "NO! PLEASE…NO!" She was shaking and sweat glistened on her face. As she slowly regained her senses, she realized that it had only been a nightmare.

Michael walked over to the table and gazed down at Sara. His smile had returned, and the pocket watch was now closed. "That seemed to be a most unpleasant experience," he said, as he picked a few grapes from the basket. "Of course, these things can be avoided. Simple compliance is the key."

Michael popped the grapes into his mouth and walked back to the doorway. He hesitated, chewing the fruit slowly, before turning back toward Sara. "I would advise you to refrain from any further outbursts."

After Michael left, the old woman went over to Sara and helped her to the bed. Sara was still shaking, and the sheet that she had draped over her body earlier was now soaked in sweat and clinging to her. "You are a foolish child! You're lucky that he only punished you. He could have taken payment!"

Sara did not respond. She had a blank expression on her face. The old woman recognized it. It was the look of the hopeless. Michael had broken her will. She dressed Sara in a long white cotton frock, and cleaned her face with a washcloth. Sara did little to help, other than to follow the old woman's instructions.

When Sara was dressed, the old woman took her hand and led her out of the cabin and down to the community building.

Sara was aware of her surroundings, but she was too paralyzed with fear to acknowledge them. Michael had power. That was very clear to her now. He had reached into her mind and plucked out the eyes of her sanity. She now knew not to resist or defy him. He had sent her on the path to hell with a simple flick of his pocket watch. There was no way she could endure these nightmares again. She knew that the next one would be worse. She would accept her role in Devil Hollow.

Michael stroked the pocket watch through his shirt as he watched Sara being led down the hill toward the community building. It had been ten years since his last wife had been lured here. Hopefully, Sara Eckels would provide him with several children, just as his other twenty-three wives had done over the decades.

CHAPTER NINETEEN

N ed watched as Sara and the old woman came down the hill and crossed over the bridge. Sara's eyes were blank and fixed, and she made no effort to look his way when he called out her name. She entered the community hall, and the door shut behind her.

"I'm afraid that your friend no longer has any interest in meeting with you, Mr. Waters."

Ned was startled by Michael's voice. He had not heard him walk on to the porch. "What do you mean?" Ned asked.

"You had hoped to sneak away with her and attempt another escape. You know perfectly well what I mean," Michael replied calmly.

Ned's eyes met Michael's gaze. He was right, of course; that is exactly what Ned's plan had been. "Look, Michael. I know you enjoy playing these little voodoo games, but I'm not falling for it today! There's nothing wrong with my knee, and your magic watch isn't going to make me think any differently. I'm leaving right now!"

Ned took two steps and felt faint. He sagged to the ground as the world seemed to spin all around him. He closed his eyes and passed out. He awoke in a cemetery next to two graves. He saw his name on one headstone. Next to his grave was another headstone that said *"LOVING WIFE"*. But there was no name on it. The deepest fear that Ned Waters had was of dying without ever knowing true love. Before him was the evidence that he had, indeed, died alone.

Ned closed his eyes and began to cry. There was an empty void in his soul that cried out for fulfillment. All Ned wanted was to have a purpose in life. He needed to fill that hole. He needed to know that his life meant something. When he opened his eyes again, he was lying on the front porch of the store.

Michael tugged at the front of his shirt and let out a light whistle. "My, it's certainly warm this morning! Take care that you do not stay too long in the sun, Mr. Waters."

"What exactly am I supposed to do all day?" Ned asked as the sweat began to bead on his forehead.

"Why, tend to the store!" Michael replied, as if surprised by the question.

"But I don't know how to do that. I'm sorry, but I don't understand what you want me to do."

Michael smiled and walked past Ned into the store. Ned followed him inside. "You simply place the produce and meats where they belong when the men bring them in every afternoon. A place for everything, and everything in its place!"

"So, what do I do while I wait for the men?"

"You relax, Mr. Waters. If someone comes in for food, you assist them. There is no need to do anything else."

Michael walked out the door without further comment, leaving Ned standing alone in the middle of the hot, stuffy, dark store. He looked around the store, and then remembered the light switch. He stood up, walked over, and flipped it on. That's when he noticed the large air-conditioning unit sticking out of the wall near the back of the store.

Within an hour of his turning the old unit on, the air inside the store had cooled tremendously. As Ned searched through the storage room, he found two old box fans. He plugged one into an electric socket and sat the other one off to the side. *This baby is going back to the cabin with me tonight!* he thought. The fan would help him sleep, and if he left the cabin door open after sundown, some cool night air could get in.

Several older women came into the store over the course of the next few hours. Ned had busied himself with memorizing where everything went. Around noon, several children came in during their lunch recess. Ned knew they would be looking for something sweet, so he showed them the rhubarb stalks. He did not keep track of who took what. He knew that the Meter Man would handle that. By early afternoon, the workers began arriving, dropping off fresh fruits, vegetables, and eggs.

At 4:55 p.m., Michael walked back into the store. He was looking at his pocket watch. "Mr. Waters, it is nearly time to ring the bell for retirement. At 5:00 p.m., all work ceases. Ring it four times."

Ned nodded eagerly and rushed to the front porch, where he grabbed the small hammer and waited. Michael smiled. "Now, Mr. Waters."

Ned Waters rang the bell loudly and with pride. Soon, the women would be arriving to gather ingredients to prepare dinner for the men. Sara and the old woman left the community building a few moments after the bell had been rung. There was no look of recognition in Ned's eyes as she passed him.

Michael stood on the bridge, pocket watch in hand, and smiled. The newest members of his little community were now in his power. He opened the watch and stared into it.

Epilogue

It wasn't until the day I saw Sara walking down the hill and pregnant that my senses returned to me. It wasn't her bulging belly that caught my eye though; it was her sunken cheeks and eyes. Sara had aged by decades in a few short years. I never let on that my sanity had returned. I had no desire to face that nightmare of loneliness again. I rose each morning at dawn and did my duties at the store. The old man I was brought here to replace passed away one month after my arrival. The old woman Sara replaced passed on two weeks later.

I had been foolish to use the air-conditioning and fans. He cannot take from you unless you take from him. It takes the new arrivals time to figure this out. Everything here is measured for payment. The food you eat, the water you drink, and the power you use, all belong to him. The prices you pay are bitter and harsh. When Michael, the Meter Man, comes to collect on your bill, it is not money he seeks, and payment is due immediately.

My first payment had become due when Michael had not been feeling very well. His face had aged considerably, and he had walked with a slight limp as he'd entered my store. He'd opened that damned watch, and I'd felt every muscle in my body contracting and cramping. The pain had been brief, but intense. An amber halo had appeared around Michael, and as it had faded, his face had slowly become younger looking. When I'd returned to my cabin that evening and seen my reflection in the bathroom mirror, I'd realized I'd aged at least ten years.

I stopped using the electricity and cut back on my eating. Still, every so often, he comes around to collect. I now understand why no one has lived past the age of fifty-five in Devil Hollow. Michael drains people of their youth, so that he can use it for himself. That pocket watch does not tell the time, it takes it. It is an instrument that both measures and punishes, but Michael decides the payment.

Sara bore him six children, two of whom died shortly after birth. The children of Devil Hollow, all sired by Michael, cannot survive long into adulthood. It seems that his cross-breeding with normal women has affected their offspring somehow. I say cross-breeding because I do not consider Michael to be human. The children age rapidly, but, unlike Michael, they cannot drain life from the humans here. Instead, they must feed upon the bodies of the elderly soon after they die. That is why the deceased are carried to the church. The bodies are tied to an altar, and the children feast upon them. The feedings make the children young for a while, but then they begin to age even faster, and they eventually die. My theory is that Michael is the son of Satan, placed here with the task of creating a race of demons. By breeding successfully with humans, his offspring could someday walk among mankind undetected.

That pocket watch is the key to his powers. Somehow, it is the meter that reads and measures our souls, providing him with the weaknesses we all possess inside. Once he has that control, we are powerless to resist. I do not believe that such a tool was created by man. Only Satan could create such an instrument of torture, and all of us who end up here are sinners. We survive because we are cowards. When faced with our greatest fears, we choose servitude over the painful nightmares.

My candle is burning low, and the flame is nearly spent. I can hear the new arrivals being led up the street in front of my cabin. I must go now and prepare the small bed in the corner. I pray that these words find you before it is too late. If you do not take measure of your own life, the Meter Man will.

THE END